# STAR WARS®
## EPISODE I
# HOW TO USE THIS BOOK

Read the captions in the eight-page booklet and, using the labels beside each sticker, choose the image that best fits in the space available.

•

Don't forget that your stickers can be placed on the page and peeled off again. If you are careful, you can use your *Star Wars*: Episode I stickers more than once.

•

You can also use the *Star Wars*: Episode I stickers to decorate your own books.

First American Edition 1999
2 4 6 8 10 9 7 5 3

Published in the United States by DK Publishing, Inc.
95 Madison Avenue
New York, New York 10016

Copyright © 1999 Lucasfilm Ltd. and TM

Written by David Pickering
Edited by Rebecca Smith and Jane Mason
Designed by Kim Browne

ISBN 0-7894-3964-6

Reproduced by Dot. Gradations, England
Printed and bound by Graphicom, Italy

**Dorling Kindersley would like to thank**
Lucasfilm for the photography

**A DK Publishing Book**
**www.dk.com**

 # Naboo

Far away from the centers of galactic power lies the peaceful planet of Naboo. Its human inhabitants live in harmony and dedicate themselves to the creation of beauty in every area of life. Their capital city, Theed, is one of the most magnificent cities in the galaxy. Beneath the surface of the planet is the fascinating society of the Gungans, an amazingly innovative amphibian race.

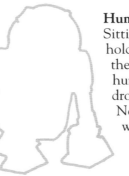

**Faithful Maiden**
The Queen is almost always surrounded by her faithful handmaidens, each of whom would risk her life for her Highness.

**Humble Droid**
Sitting in the droid hold at the back of the Queen's ship is a humble astromech droid called R2-D2. No one can guess what the future holds for him.

**Heroic Captain**
The dashing Captain Panaka is one of the Queen's most able and valued soldiers.

**Trusty Adviser**
Wise Sio Bibble is the Queen's most trusted adviser, a great support when the cares of state weigh heavily on her shoulders.

**Agile Sub**
The agile Gungan sub is designed to navigate the endless blackness of Naboo's deep waters, but it cannot always avoid their many dangers.

**Clumsy Friend**
Accident-prone Jar Jar Binks may not be the cleverest of Gungans, but he tries to do what is right and is loyal and caring; a true friend.

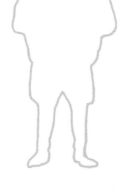

**Bossy Leader**
The tough, bossy leader of the Gungans, Boss Nass seems harsh, but he has a better side to him as well.

**Close Friend**
The handmaiden Padmé is incredibly close to young Queen Amidala and shares her innermost thoughts.

## Royal Vessel
Sleek, elegant, and fast, the Queen's Royal Starship is possibly the most beautiful spaceship in the galaxy. It has neither armor nor weapons, because it comes from a land dedicated to peace.

## Beast of Burden
These huge beasts of burden are known as Fambaas. They have been tamed by the Gungans and carry their force shield generators into battle.

## Brave Fighter
Although a planet of peace, Naboo still maintains a small army. Its soldiers are brave but few, and without much experience of battle.

## Royal Robes
The people of Naboo feel their Queen should wear the most splendid clothes and headdresses. As is fitting for a queen of an artistic people, Amidala dons exquisite gowns of striking designs.

## Queen of Naboo
The people of Naboo have chosen to democratically elect a king or queen to rule over them. Queen Amidala strives always to serve her people, respecting their laws and the advice of her counselors.

## Royal Training
Though young, Queen Amidala is wise beyond her years and has been well trained.

## Perfect Pilot
Gifted, dedicated, courageous Ric Olié has the job that every pilot dreams of: flying the Queen's Royal Starship.

## Stylish Fighter
Flown by the volunteer Royal Naboo Security Forces, the Naboo starfighter is a nimble single-pilot craft, trimmed with shiny royal chrome.

## Animal Transport
Swift and agile, Kaadus are beloved by their Gungan masters. Kaadus have strong senses of hearing and smell.

## Army Transport
Gian Speeders are the main transportation for the lightly equipped Naboo army. They resemble civilian speeders, and are just as much fun to ride!

# Dark Forces

Unknown and unsuspected, a strange alliance is about to break the long-standing peace of the Old Republic. Shadowy Lord Sidious has ordered the greedy Neimoidian Trade Federation to move from trade to conquest. Their forces have been working overtime to convert their vast trading fleet into a space navy, with a droid army inside it.

**Persistent Traders**
They trade across the galaxy, but Neimoidians are so secretive that few outsiders have any idea how their society works.

**Tough Tank**
The massive armor of this Federation AAT tank protects it from almost all attack, and its powerful armament outguns any opposition.

**Hard Workers**
Like worker ants, every one of the millions of battle droids is controlled from one central computer "brain" in the Trade Federation Droid Control Ship.

**Complex Craft**
One of the most sophisticated combat craft ever created, the droid starfighter is an actual droid, engineered to operate in deep space.

**Destroyer Droid**
Most lethal of all the Trade Federation droids, destroyer droids roll into a ball for swift travel, then uncoil to strike. Well-armed and almost indestructible, even Jedi must beware their power.

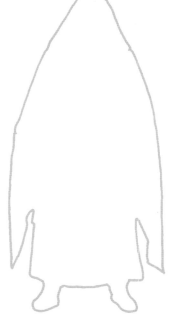

**Dark Power**
As Sith Lord and loyal apprentice of Darth Sidious, the ferocious Lord Maul is a dark shadow of a character, more lethal in battle than all but the most powerful Jedi.

# SPACECRAFT, VEHICLES, DROIDS & EQUIPMENT

Gian Speeder

Federation Troop Carrier

Battle Droid Blaster

Darth Maul's Electrobinoculars

Naboo Starfighter

Battle Droid

Queen's Royal Starship

R2-D2

Anakin's Helmet

Battle Droid Commander

Podrace Screen

Destroyer Droid

Sith Infiltrator

Neimoidian Mechno-chair

Federation AAT

# Heroes & Villains

Darth Maul

Queen Amidala

Senator Palpatine

Senate Guard

Qui-Gon Jinn

Jar Jar Binks

Rodian

Senator Bail Organa

Ric Olié

Twi'lek

Kaadu

Yoda

Queen Amidala

Boss Nass

Neimoidian

Captain Panaka

# Heroes & Villains

Sio Babble

Neimoidian

Padmé

Anakin Skywalker

Queen's Handmaiden

Sebulba

Naboo Soldier

Chancellor Valorum

Darth Sidius

Mace Windu

Obi-Wan Kenobi

Shmi Skywalker

Watto

Fambaa

Queen Amidala

Jabba the Hutt

Eopie

# SPACECRAFT, VEHICLES, DROIDS & EQUIPMENT

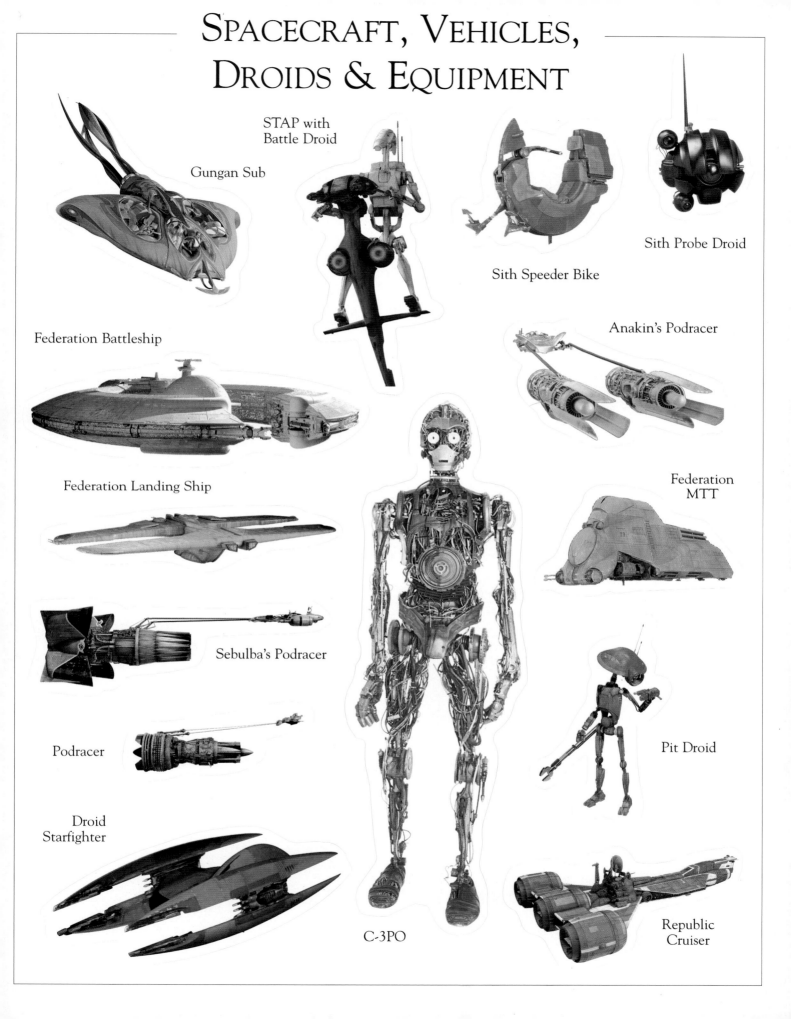

Gungan Sub

STAP with Battle Droid

Sith Speeder Bike

Sith Probe Droid

Federation Battleship

Anakin's Podracer

Federation Landing Ship

Federation MTT

Sebulba's Podracer

Podracer

Pit Droid

Droid Starfighter

C-3PO

Republic Cruiser

### Spy Ship
The ultimate spy ship, this customized Sith Infiltrator is almost undetectable. In its hold it stores sophisticated probe droids, an array of secret weapons, and the amazingly maneuverable Sith speeder bike.

### Strange Seat
Nothing illustrates the Neimoidian flair for bizarre design better than the walking chair. Intended to impress, it usually does.

### Safe Landing
Descending from orbit like mysterious flying creatures, Trade Federation landing ships carry thousands of battle droids.

### Shadowy Figure
It was thought that the Dark Lords of the Sith had vanished from the galaxy a thousand years ago, but Lord Sidious is using his dark power behind the scenes.

### Federation Carrier
This monstrous multi troop transport (MTT) ferries Federation battle droids into combat zones of all kinds.

### Secret War Freighter
In stealth and in secret, the Trade Federation has converted its fleet of huge cargo ships to carry droids and tanks instead of harmless goods to trade. Concealed weapons are ready to destroy any attempt to escape.

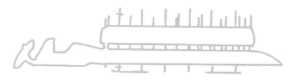

### Fast Carrier
Many of the legions of battle droids are transported on speedy troop carriers such as this one.

### Extra Vision
These electrobinoculars can detect ultra-violet, micro-movement, and heat.

### Single Carrier
The STAP (Single Trooper Ariel Platform) is designed to carry a single battle droid at high speed to terrorize scattered troops and frightened civilians, as the Trade Federation army spreads destruction far and wide.

### Lethal Weapon
Simple but lethal, the battle droid blaster is carried by every droid in the army.

# Tatooine

Wild, lawless, and oppressively hot, the desert planet Tatooine is a magnet for crooks from every corner of the galaxy. Without any government that works, its leading citizen is the infamous crimelord Jabba the Hutt. The one thing that seems to unite the planet's inhabitants is their love for Podracing – the fastest, most dangerous sport there is.

**Crimelord**
The Hutts are some of the most infamous gangsters in the galaxy, and even among that vile species, Jabba is a legend. Cunning and ruthless, murder and extortion are his daily business.

**Head Protection**
Podraces are so fast and so dangerous that no human pilots in them. Until now. Anakin Skywalker has the uncanny ability to challenge the best. This helmet is customized to his own design to optimize vision and hearing.

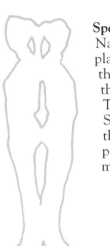

**Special Massage**
Native to the planet Ryloth in the Outer Rim, these female Twi'leks are Sebulba the Dug's personal masseuses.

**Programmed Killer**
A Sith innovation, the probe droid is programmed to find the most elusive targets, using several different scanning and surveillance systems. When a probe droid is after you, there is often no escape.

**Speedy Racer**
Anakin built this Podracer himself in his own workshop, from scrap. With numerous clever modifications, it could well be the fastest racer ever.

**Droid Service**
They look comic but are actually essential. Pit droids help maintain and service the Podracers, a truly tricky task.

**Surprise Speeder**
Although it has no weapons, shields, or sensors, the Sith speeder is a sight to fear as it is astonishingly fast and usually piloted by the dreaded Darth Maul.

**Champion Racer**
The reigning Podrace champion, Sebulba has set his heart (what there is of it) on winning the great Boonta Classic race – by fair means or foul.

**True Mother**
Enslaved by Watto on Tatooine, Shmi Skywalker asks very little for herself. Her hopes are focused entirely on her son, Anakin. Aware of his special gifts, she hopes he will one day be free.

**Bizarre Beast**
Bizarre beasts of burden, eopies are used all over Tatooine. Few take the trouble to treat them well.

**Young Force**
Gifted and popular, Anakin Skywalker is intelligent and mature beyond his years. Attuned to the Force, Anakin is the only human on Tatooine who can race Pods. But the boy dreams of one day becoming a space pilot, or even a Jedi Knight.

**View Point**
There are dozens of 3-D cameras around the Mos Espa Podrace course, feeding pictures into screens for excited fans to watch.

**Anakin's Droid**
This seemingly amateurish droid is one of Anakin's major projects. He has been building it for nearly a year, and his ingenious programming gives C-3PO capacities that no one could suspect.

**Green hunters**
The green-skinned Rodians come from the planet Rodia. They are natural fighters, and many become bounty hunters.

**Typical Pod**
This racer, like all others, is custom-built around two mighty engines and a tiny cockpit.

**Powerful Podracer**
One of the most powerful Pods ever invented, Sebulba's Podracer is also equipped with dirty tricks to sabotage rivals.

**Tough Customer**
Harsh, clever, and very, very sharp in business dealings, Watto runs a junk shop in Mos Espa on Tatooine, assisted by his slaves Anakin and Shmi Skywalker.

# Coruscant

Ancient capital of the Republic, the fabled city-planet is a byword for splendor and wealth. But something is rotten at the heart of this planet on which so many worlds depend.

**Respected Jedi**
Unconventional and a loner, Qui-Gon Jinn is none the less a highly respected and powerful Jedi Master.

**Troubled Leader**
Head of the government, Chancellor Valorum strives for good, yet is endlessly hampered by unfounded accusations and baseless scandals.

**Armed Guard**
Do not be deceived by the ceremonial uniform. The senate guards are elite troops, and lethal whether armed or not.

**Talented Pupil**
Fiery and headstrong, Obi-Wan Kenobi is a very talented Jedi Padawan. He is fiercely devoted to his Master, Qui-Gon, and together they make a good team.

**Noble Senator**
The noble Senator Bail Organa comes from Alderaan. He seems destined for high things as he battles corruption in the Senate.

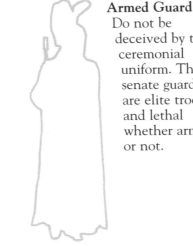

**Wise Master**
The aged Jedi Master, Yoda, is very wise and respected. Over the years he has trained many Jedi, and they look to him for guidance.

**Power seeker**
Senator Palpatine comes from Naboo. He seems well-meaning and idealistic, but secretly yearns for power.

**Senior Jedi**
A Senior Jedi on the Council, Mace Windu is wise in the ways of the Force, but believes that the Sith are extinct.

**Red Cruiser**
Assembled in the great Corellian shipyards, the red Republic Cruiser carries Jedi Knights, diplomats, and ambassadors around the galaxy.